E   00-4294

van Dort, Evelien

Am I really different

First published in 1998 by Floris Books, 15 Harrison Gardens, Edinburgh
© Text: Evelien van Dort/Christofoor Publishers, Zeist 1998
© Illustrations: Gerda Westerink/Christofoor Publishers, Zeist 1998
English version © 1998 Floris Books, Edinburgh
British Library CIP Data available ISBN 0-86315-261-9
Second impression 1999   Printed in Belgium

Am I Really Different?

A Story by Evelien van Dort
Illustrated by Gerda Westerink

Floris Books

How many spots has a ladybug or ladybird got?
Have you ever counted?

But has there ever been a ladybug with only *one* spot?
Well, yes, once upon a time ...

... there was a ladybug who had only one spot. The other ladybugs kept turning her over to find the missing spots. Some of them laughed at her.

"Go away," they said at last. "You're different from us."

So the one-spotted ladybug flew away, rather sadly.

She went to hide in the long grasses. There a worm found her and said: "What's the matter?"

"I've only got one spot," said the ladybug. "I'm different from other ladybugs and they told me to go away."

"You look fine to me," said the worm.

Soon along came an ant rolling an ant-egg. "What's the matter with you?" asked the ant.

"I've only got one spot," said the ladybug. "I'm different from other ladybugs and they told me to go away."

"You look fine to me," said the ant.

Then the ladybug had an idea.
She would go back and see
the wise old ladybug at
the top of the rose-
bush. She would
ask her if she
really was
different.

She climbed up
the rose-stem, past
all the other lady-
bugs who kept
looking at her.

When she got to the top, there
was the wise old ladybug sitting in
a beautiful rose.
"Am I really different?"
asked the one-spotted
ladybug.

"Different? Of course not. No two ladybugs are exactly the same. Everyone is different," said the wise old lady-bug. "But you're specially beautiful with your one spot."

She held up the ladybug so everyone could see how beautiful she was.

Now all the ladybugs
came to admire her and say
how lovely she was.

The ladybugs
who had laughed
at her went and
hid under a leaf,
because they felt
rather silly.

Now they realized they were *all* different, the other ladybugs flew around getting very excited and comparing their spots. And none of them was exactly the same!

That's how the ladybugs came to see that *everyone* is different — unique and special.

So are *you* really different?